This
Treasure Cove Story
belongs to

_____

**BABY SHARK AND
THE POLICE SHARKS!**

A CENTUM BOOK 978-1-913265-85-4
Published in Great Britain by Centum Books Ltd.
This edition published 2020.

1 3 5 7 9 10 8 6 4 2

Centum Books Ltd, 20 Devon Square, Newton Abbot,
Devon, TQ12 2HR, UK.

www.centumbooksltd.co.uk | books@centumbooksltd.co.uk
CENTUM BOOKS Limited Reg.No. 07641486.

A CIP catalogue record for this book is available
from the British Library.

Printed in China.

centum

A Treasure Cove Story

pinkfong
BABY SHARK
and the
Police Sharks!

Baby Shark and Daddy Shark are patrolling the ocean.
'Police Sharks on duty! We keep the peace in the ocean!' says Baby Shark.

Suddenly, a loud, wailing siren goes off and the Police Sharks hear the cry for help.

Eeeeeee!

Eeeeeee!

The Police Sharks start swinging their tails back and forth and quickly head in the direction of the siren. They are on their way to help!

The Police Sharks see someone peeking out from some coral. It is a fish family frantically flapping their fins.

'Police Sharks, thank Neptune you're here! The Octopus Sisters are fighting!'

'There's nothing to fear . . . the Police
Sharks are here!' says Baby Shark.
'Sisters, sisters, no fighting in the ocean!'
says Daddy Shark.

'We aren't fighting,' say the Octopus Sisters. 'We just got tangled up in the darkness!'

'We'll untangle you!'

The Police Sharks get straight to work.
Daddy Shark untangles one sister's arms
and Baby Shark untangles the other.

Finally, they manage to part the two sisters.
'Thank you, Police Sharks!' say the
Octopus Sisters.

'Let's high-fin, Baby Shark!'

'Over here, Police Sharks! Come quickly,' say some small fish as they gasp in horror. 'Someone has broken into Hammerhead Shark's house!'

'Help!'

The Police Sharks swim over to pull Hammerhead Shark out. 'On the count of three, Baby Shark,' says Daddy Shark. 'One . . . two . . . THREE!'

They safely pull Hammerhead
Shark out of the hole.
'I'm finally free! Thank you
so much!' says Hammerhead
Shark.

'Can't be beat, doo-doo-doo-doo-doo!'
'Task complete, doo-doo-doo-doo-doo!'

Who will the Police Sharks
help now?

There's no need to panic, the siren is sounding to start the award ceremony for the Police Sharks! 'Put your hands together for the best Police Sharks ever!' says Hammerhead Shark. 'Congratulations and thanks for keeping the peace!' say the Octopus Sisters.

Police Sharks

Treasure Cove Stories

Please contact Centum Books to receive the full list of titles in the *Treasure Cove Stories* series.
books@centumbooksltd.co.uk

Classic favourites

Recently published

Latest publications

Book list may be subject to change.